Dedication

This book is dedicated to foster families, adoptiv~~...~~, ~~...~~ families who open up their hearts and love unconditionally.

C.S.

This book is dedicated to my artistic parents who inspired me as a growing artist with their amazing talent and artwork (Mary Davies and Will Davies).

L.K.D.

Other Books Written By Connie Spanhake

Sammy and the Bully

Hermie's BIG Problem

"IT'S THE FIRST DAY OF SPRING!" Charley shouted. She jumped out of bed, "Wake up, wake up!" she yelled as she ran through the underground tunnels that made up her home.

Mom and dad yawned and stretched, "Charley it's too early, go back to bed!"

"Aww, can't I go out to play? Please?"

Mom curled back into a ball and groaned, "Fine, go play but stay out of trouble!"

"Thanks, Mom!" Charley shouted. She was very excited to finally be playing outside with her friends.

She popped her head up out of the ground and looked around hoping to find someone to play with. Everything was so quiet and still.

"IT'S THE FIRST DAY OF SPRING!" Charley shouted but she heard nothing. "Hello!" she shouted again but still nothing. She walked towards a big open field and finally she heard a sound.

A little chipmunk was squealing and darting under a log while a gray and white striped cat crept closer and closer. Its tail twitching back and forth as its silent paws slipped gracefully under the log looking for its prey. Charley ran towards the helpless chipmunk but she was too late.

The cat had swiftly grabbed the little tail and pulled him out from under the log. It was now grinning as the chipmunk hung upside down.

I'd better hurry, thought Charley as she started to run faster. Charley was just about to knock the cat off its feet when suddenly the cat curled up into a ball and they both tumbled down the hill.

Charley skidded to a stop right before they went sailing over the hill.

She wiped a tear away and turned to leave then she heard laughter. "Okay, it's my turn to catch you!" squealed the little chipmunk as she scampered back up the hill. Charley was shocked!

She hid behind a tree and watched as the two chased each other back and forth. Suddenly the chipmunk saw Charley and skidded to a stop. "Whoa," the little chipmunk said, "Who are you?"

Charley tried to act tough, "I'm Charley, who are you?"

I'm Max and this is my brother, Manny." Charley narrowed her eyes at Manny and then said, "You mean *friend* don't you? He's a cat, NOT a chipmunk." Max laughed, "No silly, he's my brother. Do you want to play with us?"

"No thanks!" Charley announced. "Chipmunks DON'T play with cats. One day your *friend* Manny is going to attack you for real. If I were you I'd find a new friend to play with."

Max crossed his arms in front of his chest, "If you can't be nice to Manny then maybe you should leave. We were doing just fine."

Charley turned around and stomped away when Max yelled, "What kind of a name is Charley for a girl anyway?

"A good name!" Charley yelled back angrily. Before Charley could say another word she heard a voice calling, "MAX, MANNY…TIME TO COME HOME!"

"Coming Momma," the two brothers yelled.

Charley hid behind a tree and watched as Manny scooped up Max and they both rolled around on the ground.

Charley turned to leave but before she could get away she heard, "Well what have we got here? Little chipmunk you look lost. Are you lost?

Charley hung her head as a tear rolled down her cheek. Max spoke up, "She's not lost, she's just mean *and* she was just leaving."

"Come here little one," Momma said, "What's your name?"
"Charley," she whispered.

Max laughed, "Yeah, Charley, what kind of name is that for a girl?"

Charley hung her head even lower.

"Is this true?" Momma asked turning to Charley.

"Yes ma'am, it is," Charley whispered turning red with embarrassment. "I didn't mean to. I thought I was saving Max from being eaten by Manny then Max said that Manny was his brother and I said that Manny could NOT be his brother."

"I see," said Momma, "What made you think Manny was going to eat Max?"

"Cats and chipmunks are enemies, everyone knows that. It's just not normal," said Charley.

"Well," said Momma looking from one to the other, "It sounds to me like a lot of wrongs need to be made right."

"Now where are your manners Max?" scolded Momma.
"Sorry Momma but *she* was being mean to Manny," said Max.

"Both of you come sit down. Let me explain something to you."
Momma looked gently at Charley and said, "We are a family. We
love each other, we support each other, and we need each other.
You may not think our family is normal Charley, but for us it's
perfectly normal. You see, when Max was born, his mom was very
sick and she asked me to take care of him. I promised her I would.
Max may not look like us but he's every bit as much of our family as
Manny is."

"I'm sorry," Charley said, "I didn't know."

"It's not important that you know the story, Charley," Momma said,
"It's important that you give others a chance and get to know them
before judging them."

Charley walked over to Manny, "Max is very lucky to have you as a brother. It was wrong of me to judge you. I'm very sorry."

Momma looked at Max, "Max do you have something to say to Charley?" Max's cheeks turned pink then he looked at Charley and said, "I'm sorry." for making fun of your name."

"That's okay," Charley replied, "My real name is Charlotte but my friends call me Charley." Charley looked down at her feet and said shyly, "I would really like it if you and Manny would call me Charley."

Momma smiled and said, "That sounds like a terrific idea. Now you three go on and play until lunch is ready."

"Yes, Momma," they all said laughing as the three friends ran off to play.

Made in the USA
Monee, IL
17 December 2019

18963531R00017